MONSTER By Mistake!

Tracy's Magic Show

www.monsterbymistake.com

Created by
Mark Mayerson

Adapted by
Paul Kropp

Graphics by Studio 345

WINDING STAIR
PRESS

an Imprint of Stewart House Publishing Inc.

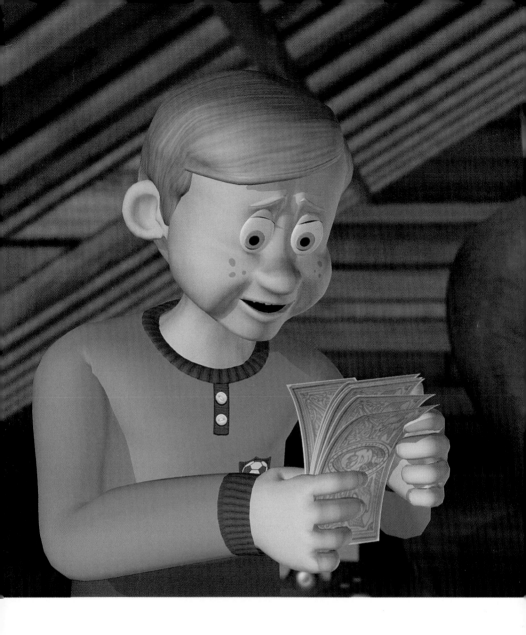

Warren wanted to buy a new computer game.

Tracy had a little money.
But it was still not enough.

Johnny the Ghost had a good idea.
"You and your sister could do a magic show."

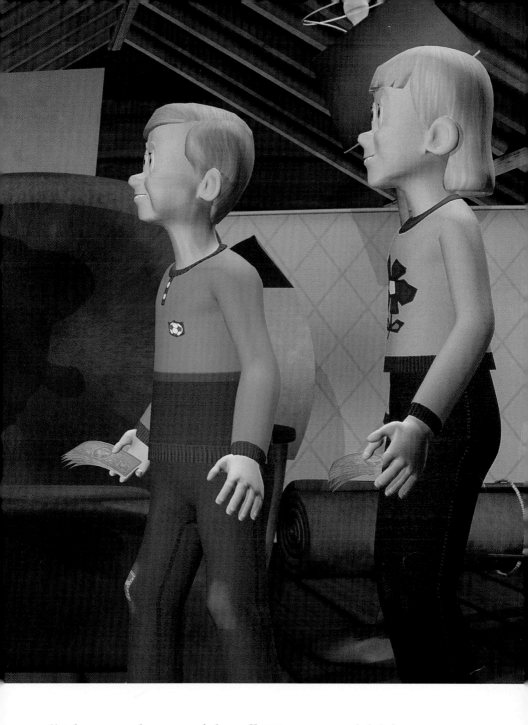

"I have a better idea," Warren told him.

He sneezed. "The Monster can be in the magic show, too!"

The Monster and Tracy put up posters.

A lady asked them to put on a magic show
for her son.

She really liked the Monster.

Tracy and the Monster were happy
to get the job.

They got to the house just in time.

Tracy did a magic trick.

But the boy did not care.

Tracy made some toys fly in the air.

But the boy did not care.

Warren turned into the Monster.
He played his trumpet.

But the boy did not care.

Tracy got mad. "I'll try some real magic!" she said.

Tracy used the magic jewel and
the Book of Spells.

Kazap! The magic spell hit an action toy.

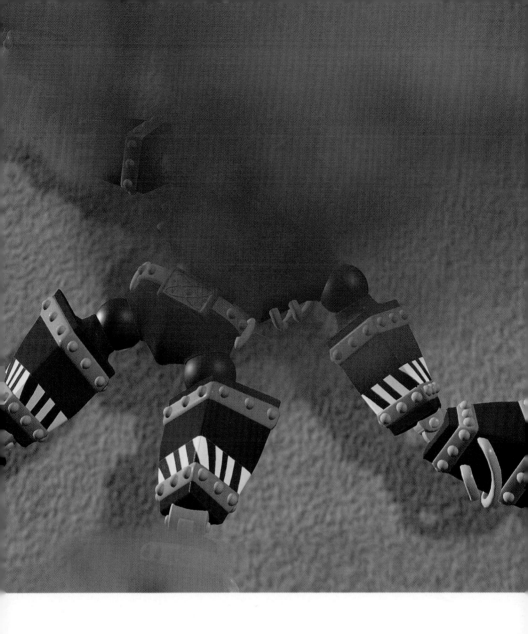

The action toy fell to the ground.
But then ....

It turned into a giant!

"I am the King of the Universe!"

"That is a great trick," the boy said.

"Now this is fun!"

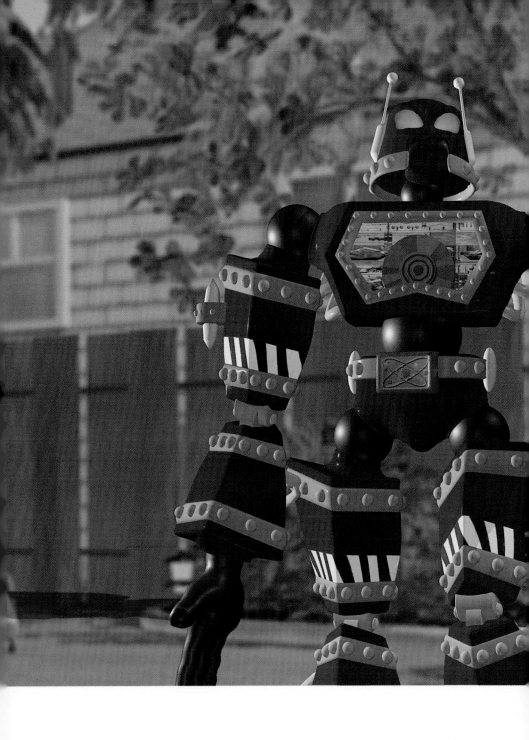

Tracy and the Monster were worried.

"I will have to change him back,"
Tracy said.

Kazoom! The King of the Universe was
a toy again.

"Wow! Can you do more magic tricks?"
the boy asked.

Note to parents and teachers about Monster By Mistake Readers:

We trust your young readers will enjoy developing their reading skills with these great stories. Here is a simple guide to help you choose the right level for your child:

Level One Monster Readers
These stories are carefully written to build the confidence of beginning readers. They have been written to North American curriculum standards for Grade 1.

Featuring:
- short, simple sentences
- easy-to-recognize words
- exciting images to support the story

Level Two Monster Readers
Designed to build confidence of a new reader. They have been written to North American curriculum standards for Grade 2.

Featuring:
- slightly more difficult vocabulary
- more complex sentence and story structures
- exciting images to support the story

Level Three: Chapter books
Designed to appeal to both the advanced reader and the reluctant reader. They have been written to North American curriculum standards for Grades 3 and 4.

Featuring:
- complete plots based on the television episode
- controlled vocabulary and general readability
- stories deal with real life issues such as bullying, self-esteem and problem solving

Our Educational Consultant, Paul Kropp, is an author, editor and educator. His work includes young adult novels, novels for reluctant readers and the bestselling resource *How to Make Your Child a Reader for Life*. Visit his website: www.paulkropp.com

Text © by Winding Stair
Graphics © 2002 by Monster By Mistake Enterprises Ltd.

Monster By Mistake Series is produced by
CCI Entertainment Ltd. and Catapult Productions
Series Executive Producers: Arnie Zipursky and
Kim Davidson
Based on the Screenplay "Entertainling Orville"
by Cathy Moss

Text Design: Counterpunch
Cover Design: Darrin La Framboise

All rights reserved.

1 2 3 4 5 6   07 06 05 04 03 02

Printed and bound in Canada

Contact Stewart House Publishing
at info@stewarthousepub.com or 1-866-474-3478

National Library of Canada Cataloguing in Publication

Mayerson, Mark
    Tracey's magic show / created by Mark Mayerson;
adapted by Paul Kropp.

(Monster by mistake)
Based on an episode of the television program, Monster
by mistake.
Level 2.
For use in grades 1–2.
ISBN 1-55366-318-7

    I. Kropp, Paul, 1948– II. Catapult (Firm), III. Title.
IV. Series.

PS8576.A8685T73 2002   jC813'.6   C2002-903659-3
PZ7